Chloe the Topaz Fairy

by Daisy Meadows

illustrated by Georgie Ripper

Join the Rainbow Magic Reading Challenge!

Read the story and collect your fairy points to climb the Reading Rainbow online. Turn to the back of the book for details!

This book is worth 5 points.

The Fairyland Palace

Adventure Playground

Tippington Manor

Tippington Town

The Tall Toy Store

Fountain

The Jewel Fairies

To Rachel and Anna Prockter,
two fairy friends

Special thanks to
Linda Chapman

ORCHARD BOOKS

First published in Great Britain in 2005 by Orchard Books
This edition published in 2016 by The Watts Publishing Group

3 5 7 9 10 8 6 4 2

© 2016 Rainbow Magic Limited.
© 2016 HIT Entertainment Limited.
Illustrations © Georgie Ripper 2005

HiT entertainment

The moral rights of the author and illustrator have been asserted.

A CIP catalogue record for this book is available from the British Library.

ISBN 978 1 40834 875 8

Printed in Great Britain

MIX
Paper from
responsible sources
FSC® C104740

The paper and board used in this book are made from wood from responsible sources

Orchard Books
An imprint of Hachette Children's Group
Part of The Watts Publishing Group Limited
Carmelite House, 50 Victoria Embankment, London EC4Y 0DZ

An Hachette UK Company
www.hachette.co.uk
www.hachettechildrens.co.uk

By Frosty magic I cast away
These seven jewels with their fiery rays,
So their magic powers will not be felt
And my icy castle shall not melt.

The fairies may search high and low
To find the gems and take them home.
But I will send my goblin guards
To make the fairies' mission hard.

Contents

Goblins in Disguise!

"There's a fancy dress shop!"
Kirsty Tate said, pointing at one
of the shops on Cherrywell's busy
high street.

"Brilliant!" Rachel Walker replied
happily. "Let's go and choose
costumes for Isabel's Halloween
party before the bus arrives."

"OK," Kirsty agreed. She was staying at Rachel's house for half-term week and the girls had just been bowling with some of Rachel's friends from school. One of them, Isabel, had invited everyone to a Halloween party at the weekend. "What do you want to dress up as?" Kirsty asked Rachel.

"Something magical, of course!" Rachel replied with a grin.

Kirsty smiled back. She and Rachel loved magic. It was because they shared an amazing secret: they were friends with the fairies!

Their magical adventures had started one summer when the girls had helped the fairies stop Jack Frost from taking the colour away from Fairyland. Since then, the Fairy King and Queen had asked for their help several times. In fact, that very week, Rachel and Kirsty were right in the middle of another fairy adventure, because Jack Frost was causing trouble again!

This time he'd stolen seven sparkling jewels from Queen Titania's tiara. The jewels were very precious because they controlled special fairy powers, like the fairies' ability to fly, or to give children in the human world sweet dreams. Every year, in a special celebration, the fairies would recharge their wands with the jewels' magic. This year's ceremony was due to take place in just a few days' time.

If the gems weren't found by then, the fairies would run out of the jewels' special magic completely!

Jack Frost had hoped to keep the magic jewels himself. But when their magical light had started to melt his ice castle, he had flown into a rage and cast a spell to hurl the gems into the human world. Then he sent his mean goblin servants to guard them so that the fairies couldn't get them back.

Rachel and Kirsty had already helped three of the Jewel Fairies recover their magic gems, but there were still four jewels left to find.

"Do you think we'll find another jewel today?" Rachel whispered as she and Kirsty ran up to the shop.

"I hope so," Kirsty replied.

A small boy and his mum were looking at the display in the window of the fancy dress shop. There were bright orange Halloween banners, pumpkin lanterns and two shop dummies wearing children's Halloween costumes – one dressed as a witch and one as a goblin.

Suddenly the boy gasped. "Mum! Did you see that?" he cried. "The model in that goblin costume moved!"

Rachel and Kirsty stopped and stared at each other.

"Don't be silly, Tom," the boy's mum laughed, leading him away. "Come along."

"A goblin model that moved?" Kirsty hissed to Rachel. "We'd better have a look."

They peered closely at the window display. The dummy the boy had pointed out was wearing a green goblin costume and a little red pointed hat. But Rachel's eyes widened as she took in the goblin's beady eyes, long nose and great big feet.

"That's not a goblin costume!" she exclaimed. "It's a *real* goblin in a tunic and a hat!"

"And look at the witch," Kirsty added.
The witch model sported a long
black skirt, a pointed hat
and a broomstick, but its
lumpy green nose and
warty chin looked
distinctly goblin-like to her.

"The witch is a goblin,
too!" Rachel gasped.

A thought hit Kirsty and she clutched at
Rachel's arm in excitement. "Oh, Rachel,
if there are goblins in the window, maybe
one of the fairies' magic jewels is inside
the shop!"

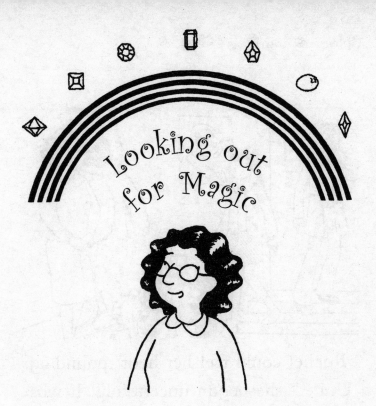

Looking out for Magic

"Come on. Let's go and see!" Rachel urged.

Pushing the door open, the girls hurried down three stone steps into the shop. An assistant came bustling to meet them. She had curly brown hair and a cheerful face. "Hello," she said, stepping around a large pile of pumpkin lanterns near the door. "Can I help you?"

Rachel could feel her heart pounding. "Um…" she began uncertainly. It was hard to concentrate knowing that there were two goblins standing just a few feet away.

"Could we look at some costumes please?" Kirsty put in quickly. "We're going to a Halloween party at the weekend and we haven't got anything to wear."

The shop assistant smiled. "Well, you've come to the right place! My name's Maggie and I'm sure I can sort you both out with something. What did you have in mind?"

"I think I'd..." Kirsty looked around and saw a display of cat costumes. "I think I'd like to try a cat costume, please," she decided.

"Well we have lots of those in for Halloween," replied Maggie. "How about you, my dear?' she asked Rachel.

Rachel thought fast. They needed to search the shop for the jewel. If Kirsty could keep Maggie busy, then maybe she could look around. "I haven't quite decided yet," she replied truthfully. "Would it be all right if I just have a look first?"

"Of course," Maggie answered. "You go ahead." She smiled at Kirsty. "Now, why don't you come to the changing rooms with me and I'll find a cat costume in your size?"

As Kirsty headed off with Maggie, Rachel glanced round the shop. There were rails of costumes, and shelves piled high with wigs, make-up and masks. Rachel noticed a container full of plastic swords and a stand hung with fairy-like wings and wands. If there is a magic jewel in this shop, she thought, it could be anywhere!

Her eyes fell on a pirate display near the back of the shop. There were two dummies dressed in pirate costumes, each with an eye-patch, standing on a desert island. Between the pirates stood a palm tree and a huge treasure chest, with gold chains and strings of pearls spilling from it. *That would be the perfect place for a jewel to hide,* Rachel thought, hurrying over to the treasure chest.

As she drew closer, her heart seemed to skip a beat. The chest was glowing with a deep golden light. *Magic!* Rachel thought, looking at the way the metal chains glittered and gleamed in the light. It has to be! Holding her breath, she lifted the heavy lid of the chest.

Suddenly, a fountain of orange and gold sparkles shot into the air. Rachel gasped and nearly dropped the lid, for twirling in the middle of the sparkles was a tiny fairy dressed in beautiful, fiery colours!

Costumes Galore!

"Hello!" cried the fairy brightly. She was wearing a yellow skirt with three frills at the bottom, an orange wrap-around top and tiny sparkling orange shoes. Her long, black, wavy hair was held back by a red hairband.

"Hi!" Rachel replied in delight. She thought she recognised the fairy.

"You're Chloe the Topaz Fairy, aren't
you?"

Chloe nodded. "That's right."

Rachel glanced over her shoulder.
Luckily, Maggie was too busy handing
clothes to Kirsty to have noticed
anything. Rachel led Chloe behind a
costume rail. "Is your Topaz in this
shop?" she asked. "Kirsty and I thought
there might be a magic jewel in here."

"The magic Topaz is definitely in here. I can feel it," Chloe responded, perching on Rachel's hand. "But I haven't been able to find it. I was searching the treasure chest when the lid fell shut, and I was trapped inside. Thanks for rescuing me."

"That's OK," Rachel declared with a smile. She peeped around the side of the rail. "Have you seen the goblins?"

Chloe looked alarmed. "Goblins! What goblins?"

"There are two in the window pretending to be shop dummies," Rachel explained.

Chloe shivered. "They must be here to guard the Topaz. We'll have to try and send it back to Fairyland without them noticing."

"Yes," Rachel agreed. "But we need to find it first. Where shall we start looking?" Just then she heard the

changing-room curtains being pulled back. She peered round the clothes rail to see how her friend was getting on. "That cat costume fits you just fine," Maggie was saying to Kirsty. "But you need some ears. Just wait there while I get you some from the stockroom."

As Maggie moved away, Rachel hurried over. "Kirsty!" she hissed.

"What is it?" Kirsty asked eagerly. "Have you found something? Oh!" she gasped, as she saw Chloe fluttering beside Rachel.

The little fairy grinned. "Hi, I'm Chloe," she said.

"Chloe's Topaz is somewhere in here," Rachel told Kirsty quietly. "We've got to find it!"

"What does it look like?" Kirsty asked.

"It's a deep golden colour," Chloe replied. "And it controls changing magic, so keep your eyes open for any strange changes."

"It might be hidden among those
fairy wands," Rachel
suggested, pointing
to a display near
the till. "Let's
check there."

"You do that
while I check the
queen costume," Kirsty

said, pointing to an outfit
near the window. It
was a beautiful,
jewelled dress
and cloak,
with a crown
set with more
glittering gems.
"The Topaz could
easily hide there."

Rachel's sharp ears caught the sound of footsteps. "Maggie's coming back!" she warned, and she and Chloe slipped behind the costume rail again.

"Let's check the fairy display," Rachel whispered to Chloe. "If you hide in the pocket of my coat, Maggie won't see you."

Chloe dived into Rachel's pocket and they headed over to the magic wands.

Meanwhile, Maggie was handing the cat ears to Kirsty.

"Um," Kirsty began, "I'm really sorry, but I've just spotted the queen costume, and it's so beautiful! Would you mind if I tried that one on instead?"

"Of course not!" Maggie replied cheerfully. "I'll fetch it for you." She bustled over to the shop window and took the costume off the dummy. "Here we are!" she said, heading back to Kirsty with the costume in her arms.

As Maggie carried the costume past the window, Kirsty heard a faint pop, and saw the air behind Maggie shimmer with a golden glow. Then, to Kirsty's amazement, the witch costume on the goblin in the window changed to a suit of armour! Kirsty gasped and looked around quickly for her friends. She felt certain that the costume change must be the work of Chloe's magic Topaz!

All Change

Maggie drew closer to Kirsty. Behind her, the goblins in the window turned around in confusion. The metal visor on the helmet of the suit of armour fell down with a dull clunk, and the goblin inside let out a muffled shriek of surprise.

Hearing the noise, Maggie swung round. She stared at the suit of armour curiously.

"Where did that come from?" she murmured. "I thought there was a witch costume in the window." She turned back to Kirsty. "Did you see a witch costume?"

Kirsty didn't know what to say. "Um, I can't really remember," she replied.

"Maybe the window dresser changed the costumes yesterday. That was my day off," Maggie explained. "But I'm surprised I didn't notice!"

Behind Maggie, Kirsty could see the
goblin in the red hat
silently sniggering
at his friend, who
was now struggling
to yank open the
heavy visor of his helmet.

Meanwhile, Maggie was shaking out
the queen costume for Kirsty to try on.
As she did so, there was a second faint
pop. Kirsty looked around nervously.

 This time she saw the
air shimmer red,
and the bow
and arrows on
a nearby Robin
Hood costume
turned into a
set of bagpipes!

Kirsty's hand flew to her mouth. She hoped Maggie wouldn't notice. She had no idea how she would explain why Robin Hood was clutching the bagpipes! She bit her lip as all the earrings on a display to Maggie's left suddenly turned into pink-and-white stripy sweets. *The Topaz must be in the things that Maggie is holding!* Kirsty thought.

Suddenly, she saw the goblin in armour step cautiously out of the window. He had got his visor open now and his beady eyes were fixed on the robes in Maggie's arms. *Oh no!* Kirsty thought, realising that the goblin must have seen the magic working too.

She watched anxiously as the goblin inched slowly towards Maggie. But, as he did so, one of his big feet knocked into the container of plastic swords.

The rattle made Maggie swing round.

Grabbing a sword, the goblin froze as if he was just another shop display.

"Thanks for the costume," Kirsty said, stepping forward to distract Maggie. "Can I try it on now?"

Throwing the suit of armour a puzzled glance, Maggie turned back to Kirsty. "Of course," she replied, helping Kirsty into the dress and draping the cloak around her shoulders.

As Kirsty took the crown, she noticed a huge golden stone in the centre of it. It seemed to shimmer and shine. Was it the magic Topaz? Kirsty put the crown on, and immediately her head started to tingle with fairy magic. "Oh, wow!" she breathed.

"Do you like it?" Maggie smiled.
"I think I've got a sceptre in the
stockroom that would look lovely with
that costume. I'll see if I can find it
for you."

As soon as Maggie had gone, Kirsty
turned to Rachel and Chloe who were
at the fairy display. "I've got the
Topaz!" she called softly.

"Hooray!" Rachel
exclaimed.

"Where is it?"
asked Chloe,
zooming out
of Rachel's
pocket in a
whoosh of sparks.

"In the crown on
my head!" replied Kirsty.

Rachel looked at Kirsty's head in surprise. "Crown?" she asked. "Do you mean the turban?"

Curiously, Kirsty turned to look in the changing-room mirror. Immediately, she saw that the crown had changed into a turban, but the golden Topaz still glittered at its centre. "It's changed!" she breathed.

At that moment, Rachel let out a cry of alarm. "Kirsty!"

"Watch out!" Chloe exclaimed at the same time.

Kirsty whirled round to see that the goblin in armour had crept up on her while she wasn't looking. Now, cackling gleefully, he gave a great leap and snatched the turban and the Topaz right off Kirsty's head!

Stop that Goblin!

"I've got the Topaz!" the goblin
shouted, staggering down the shop
with the turban and its precious,
glowing jewel.

"After him!" Kirsty cried, as the
goblin charged towards the shop door,
his metal armour clanking.

Rachel and Chloe raced after him.

"Come on!" the goblin in the red hat shouted, running up the steps towards the door. But the armour wasn't easy for his friend to run in. The visor fell down over his eyes again and, unable to see anything, he bumped clumsily into the pile of Halloween lanterns, sending them bouncing and rolling across the floor.

The goblin tripped over one of them and lost his balance. "Whaaaa!" he cried, tumbling onto his back among the pumpkins. As he fell, the turban slipped from his grasp and flew through the air.

"You slug-brained idiot!" the other goblin spluttered. "What do you think you are doing?"

"I can't see," the armoured goblin whined, trying to tug his visor up. "And now I've hurt my bottom!"

"Catch that turban, Rachel!" Kirsty exclaimed, as the turban plummeted towards the ground.

Rachel reached for it, but missed. As the turban hit the ground, the Topaz was jolted out of its setting. Bouncing across the floor, the golden gem rolled straight in amongst the scattered pumpkins. There was a loud pop, a shimmer of golden light and, in the blink of an eye, all the pumpkins had changed into pineapples!

"Where's the Topaz?" Kirsty cried,
lifting the hem of her
costume and running over.

"I can see it!"
Chloe gasped,
swooping towards
the pineapples
and pointing
with her wand.

Kirsty saw the
Topaz glowing
amongst the fruit.
But as Chloe zoomed
towards it, the goblin
by the door saw it too.
Sliding through the
pineapples as if he was on
ice, he scooped the Topaz up with one
hand just before Chloe reached it.

"Ow!" he wailed as the heat of the magic jewel burnt his icy goblin skin.

For a moment, Kirsty felt a burst of hope. She remembered that goblins couldn't touch the magic jewels with their bare hands without getting burnt. She waited for the goblin to drop the Topaz.

But instead there was another loud pop, and the goblin's tunic and hat changed into a teddy-bear costume, complete with furry gloves that looked like paws!

"I've got the Topaz!" the teddy-bear
goblin shouted triumphantly to his
friend, who was scrambling out of his
metal armour. "Let's get out of here!"
Clutching the jewel in his furry paws,
he charged back towards the door.

Chloe swooped at the teddy-bear
goblin's head. "Give me my jewel!"
she cried.

"Shan't!" he shouted rudely. "The
Topaz isn't yours anymore. It's ours, and
you're never going to get it back!"

"Come on, Kirsty!" Rachel cried. "We've
got to stop them!"

She and Kirsty began to run through the
pineapples, trying not to trip on the fruit.
The goblins had reached the steps. Rachel
was horrified to see that they were going
to get away with the Topaz. But then,
suddenly, she had an idea. She picked up

a pineapple as if it was a bowling ball, and then, with a thrust of her arm, she sent it whizzing along the floor – straight at the two goblins.

The pineapple hit the feet of the goblin who had been in armour. He cried out in surprise and grabbed the arm of the teddy-bear goblin who was halfway up the steps. For a moment, both goblins teetered on the steps, arms flailing, and then they toppled down the stairs to land in a heap.

The Topaz was flung from the goblin's furry paw and went spinning through the air. As it flew past the lights there was a pop, the air shimmered with an amber glow and suddenly all the shop lights became tiny round disco balls that dazzled and shone with magic.

Chloe plunged after the jewel, and caught it in both hands. But it was too heavy for her to fly with. "Whoa!" she cried in alarm, her wings fluttering frantically.

She and the jewel sank towards
the ground. "Help!"
Seeing what was
happening, Kirsty
scrambled to her feet
and dived towards
the fairy with her
hands outstretched.
The fairy and the
Topaz landed
safely in her palms.
Kirsty pulled her
hands to her chest,
her heart beating fast.
Was Chloe OK?
"Phew!" Chloe said,
poking her head out of
Kirsty's cupped hands and grinning.
"Thanks for catching me, Kirsty!"

"Are you all right?" Rachel asked, scrambling over and looking at her in concern.

"I'm fine," Chloe replied. Her hair was standing on end, but her brown eyes were sparkling. "In fact, I'm better than fine," she said, looking at the groaning goblins, "now that I've got my Topaz back!"

Just then, there was a noise from the stockroom. "I've found the sceptre!" came Maggie's cheerful voice. "I'll be out in a minute, once I've put these boxes away."

"Oh, no!" Rachel gasped in horror. "I'd forgotten about Maggie." She looked around at the shop. There were pineapples all over the floor, glittering mirror balls instead of lights, and bits of armour scattered everywhere – not to mention the fact that the window display was ruined because its two main stars were in a heap by the door!

"Maggie will be horrified by all this mess!" Kirsty said.

"Don't worry," Chloe replied cheerfully. "Now I've got the Topaz back, I can work some changing magic." She touched her golden wand to the Topaz in Kirsty's hand.

The tip of the wand began to gleam like a ray of sparkling sunshine. Lifting it high in the air, the little fairy waved it expertly.

There was a quick series of pops, like popcorn bursting in a pan, and everything started to change again. The air glimmered orange, then red, and finally gold, as the pineapples changed back to pumpkins, the disco lights changed to normal lights, two proper shop dummies appeared in the window and everything was magically back the way it had been in the first place. Even the bits of armour were neatly on a shelf. With a final loud pop, all the bits of armour jumped neatly onto a shelf.

"Phew!" Rachel said in relief.

Chloe smiled at her. "It's all back to normal."

"Except for one thing," Kirsty said slowly, looking at the door. "What's Maggie going to say when she sees those goblins?"

Fluffy Bunnies

The goblins were picking themselves up off the floor, groaning and arguing. Their costumes had disappeared and they were back to their ordinary, green goblin selves.

"Why did you trip me up like that?" the first goblin demanded.

"Why did you let the Topaz go?"

spluttered the other. "Butterfingers!"

"Don't call me butterfingers!" the
first goblin shouted.

"Oh, dear, I think those two are
going to take some explaining,"
Rachel said.

"Leave it to me!" Chloe flew over

to the goblins.
"Pesky fairy!"
snarled the first
goblin, making a
swipe at Chloe,
who darted easily
out of his way. "Give
us the Topaz back!"

"No," Chloe replied
coolly. "And my wand is charged
up with changing magic now, so
I can turn you into anything I like!"

She smiled. "And if you don't leave the shop this minute, I'm going to turn you both into fluffy, pink bunny rabbits!"

The goblins' mouths dropped open in horror.

"Bunny rabbits!" the first one exclaimed. "Yuck!"

"You wouldn't!" said the second.

Chloe grinned. "Oh yes I would." She shot a look at Rachel and Kirsty.

"What do you two think?"

Rachel grinned back. "I think they'd make lovely bunny rabbits," she said.

"Especially fluffy pink ones," Kirsty added.

Chloe lifted her wand.

"Noooooo!" both goblins cried in alarm, and they turned and ran up the steps. Fighting each other out of the way, they yanked the shop door open and disappeared down the high street at top speed.

Rachel, Kirsty and Chloe
burst out laughing.

"You girls seem
to be having a
good time,"
Maggie said,
emerging from
the stockroom with
a sceptre in her hand.

Chloe darted into Rachel's
pocket just in time.

"I'm sorry I was so long," Maggie added,
looking at the door which was swinging
open. "Have I missed a customer?"

"It's OK," said Kirsty, quickly putting
the Topaz back in her pocket. "It was
just, er..."

"Someone looking for pineapples,"
Rachel finished quickly.

Kirsty hid a grin as Maggie looked at Rachel in surprise. "Pineapples?" she queried.

Rachel nodded. "When they realised you didn't sell any, they left," she added.

"Oh, right." Maggie blinked. "Well, never mind. Here's the sceptre," she said, handing it to Kirsty. She turned to Rachel. "Have you decided on your costume yet?"

"I think I'd like to go as a fairy," Rachel replied. "You've got some lovely fairy wings and wands."

"Yes," Kirsty agreed, handing the sceptre back carefully. "Thank you for letting me try the costumes on, but I think I'd like to go as a fairy too." She saw Chloe's head pop out of Rachel's pocket. The fairy grinned and gave her a thumbs-up sign before quickly ducking down so Maggie wouldn't see her.

Kirsty changed out of the Queen's costume and the girls chose a pair of wings and a wand each. Just as they

finished paying for them the phone
rang. "Enjoy your Halloween party,
girls," Maggie said as she hurried off to
answer the call.

The moment she was gone, Chloe

flew out of Rachel's
pocket in a cloud
of fairy dust. "I
wish I could stay
and see you off to
your party. I bet
you'll look great
in your fairy
costumes, but I'd
better get back to
Fairyland now. Thank you
for helping me rescue the Topaz."
Kirsty took the stone out of her pocket.
"Here it is," she said, holding it out.

Chloe touched her wand to the golden jewel, and in a fountain of orange sparkles it disappeared safely back to Fairyland.

Rachel and Kirsty picked up their shopping bags containing their wings and wands and headed out of the shop.

"See you soon!" Chloe said as Rachel pulled the door open.

"Bye," the girls called as the little fairy spun round in a swirl of golden light and then zoomed away.

"I'm glad we were able to help her," Rachel said happily.

"Me too," Kirsty agreed. A sparkle near the ceiling caught her eye, and she looked up curiously. A single tiny disco ball was still hanging there, glittering and shining with fairy magic. "Look!" she exclaimed. "Chloe left one little mirror ball behind."

Rachel laughed. "There'll always be magic in the shop now," she said. Then she spotted the bus turning into the high street. "Come on!" she gasped, pulling the door shut behind them. "We've got to catch the bus, Kirsty!"

They began to run down the street.
"It's been an amazing day, hasn't it?"
Kirsty panted. "What do you think will
happen tomorrow?"

"I don't know," Rachel said, as they reached the bus stop just in time and jumped on board. She grinned at Kirsty. "But it's bound to be something magic!

**Now Rachel and Kirsty
must help...**

Amy the Amethyst Fairy

Read on for a sneak peek...

"Kirsty, we're here!" Rachel Walker announced, looking out of the car window and pointing at a large sign on the wall which read *Welcome to Tippington Manor.*

Kirsty Tate, Rachel's best friend, was peering up at the cloudy sky. "I hope it's not going to rain," she said anxiously. Then the house itself caught her eye. "Oh, look, Rachel, there's the house! Isn't it lovely?"

At the bottom of the long, sweeping gravel drive stood Tippington Manor, a

huge Victorian house with an enormous
wooden door, rows of tall windows and
ivy rambling all over its old red bricks.
The house was surrounded by gardens full
of flowers and spreading trees, their autumn
leaves glowing in shades of red and gold.

"Look over there, Kirsty," Rachel said to
her friend as Mr Walker turned into the
car park. "An adventure playground!"

Kirsty looked in the direction Rachel
was pointing, and was delighted to spy
the playground on a hill behind
the house. She could see some tyres
dangling on ropes, a silver slide and what
looked like a big wooden tree-house in the
centre, built around a towering oak tree.

"Isn't it great?" Kirsty whispered to
Rachel, as they climbed out of the car.
"The fairies would love that tree-house!"

Rachel grinned and nodded. She and Kirsty were the only people in the world who were friends with the fairies! Whenever there was trouble in Fairyland the two girls tried to help sort things out.

The fairies' biggest trouble-maker was cold, icy Jack Frost, who had recently stolen the seven magic jewels from the Queen of Fairyland's tiara. Because these gems controlled much of the magic in Fairyland, greedy Jack Frost had wanted them for himself. But when the glowing heat and light of the jewels had begun to melt his ice castle, Jack Frost had flung them out into the human world in a fit of rage...

Read Amy the Amethyst Fairy to find out what adventures are in store for Kirsty and Rachel!

Meet the
Jewel Fairies

Join Rachel and Kirsty as they hunt for the
jewels that naughty Jack Frost has stolen
from Queen Titania's crown!

www.rainbowmagicbooks.co.uk

Calling all parents, carers and teachers!
The Rainbow Magic fairies are here to help
your child enter the magical world of reading.
Whatever reading stage they are at, there's
a Rainbow Magic book for everyone!
Here is Lydia the Reading Fairy's guide to
supporting your child's journey at all levels.

Starting Out

1. Our Rainbow Magic Beginner Readers are perfect for first-time readers who are just beginning to develop reading skills and confidence. Approved by teachers, they contain a full range of educational levelling, as well as lively full-colour illustrations.

Developing Readers

2. Rainbow Magic Early Readers contain longer stories and wider vocabulary for building stamina and growing confidence. These are adaptations of our most popular Rainbow Magic stories, specially developed for younger readers in conjunction with an Early Years reading consultant, with full-colour illustrations.

Going Solo

3. The Rainbow Magic chapter books – a mixture of series and one-off specials – contain accessible writing to encourage your child to venture into reading independently. These highly collectible and much-loved magical stories inspire a love of reading to last a lifetime.

www.rainbowmagicbooks.co.uk

"Rainbow Magic got my daughter reading chapter books. Great sparkly covers, cute fairies and traditional stories full of magic that she found impossible to put down" – Mother of Edie (6 years)

"Florence LOVES the Rainbow Magic books. She really enjoys reading now" Mother of Florence (6 years)

The Rainbow Magic Reading Challenge

Well done, fairy friend – you have completed the book!
This book was worth 5 points.

See how far you have climbed on the **Reading Rainbow**
on the Rainbow Magic website below.

The more books you read, the more points you will get,
and the closer you will be to becoming a Fairy Princess!

How to get your Reading Rainbow
1. Cut out the coin below
2. Go to the Rainbow Magic website
3. Download and print out your poster
4. Add your coin and climb up the Reading Rainbow!

There's all this and lots more at
www.rainbowmagicbooks.co.uk

You'll find activities, competitions, stories, a special
newsletter and complete profiles of all the
Rainbow Magic fairies. Find a fairy with your name!